A FINE, FINE SCHOOL

BY SHARON CREECH

PICTURES BY HARRY BLISS

SCHOLASTIC INC.

New York Toronto London Auckland Sydney
Mexico City New Delhi Hong Kong Buenos Aires

ISBN 0-439-41797-X

Text copyright © 2001 by Sharon Creech.
Illustrations copyright © 2001 by Harry Bliss.
All rights reserved. Published by Scholastic Inc.,
557 Broadway, New York, NY 10012, by arrangement with
Joanna Cotler Books, an imprint of HarperCollins Publishers.
SCHOLASTIC and associated logos are trademarks and/or
registered trademarks of Scholastic Inc.

12 11 10 9 8 7 6 5 4 3 2 1   2 3 4 5 6 7/0

Printed in the U.S.A.   24

First Scholastic printing, September 2002

Typography by Alicia Mikles

For Lyle: A fine, fine headmaster
—S.C.

For Bill Peet and my fine, fine son, Alexander
—H.B.

Mr. Keene was a principal who loved his school. Every morning he strolled down the hallway and saw the children in their classes. He saw them learning shapes and colors and numbers and letters. He saw them reading and writing and drawing and painting. He saw them making dinosaurs and forts and pyramids.

"Oh!" he would say. "Aren't these fine children? Aren't these fine teachers? Isn't this a fine, fine school?"

FUTURISM ...ISM CUBISM IMPRESSIONIS...

THE ISMS

PICASSO REWALD

SUZY

Near Mr. Keene's school, Tillie lived with her parents and her brother and her dog, Beans, in a small house next to a big tree.

On Mondays and Tuesdays and Wednesdays and Thursdays and Fridays, Tillie went off to school.

At school, Tillie learned her shapes and colors and numbers and letters. Sometimes, when she saw Mr. Keene standing in the hallway, he waved.

"Aren't these fine children?" he said to himself. "Aren't these fine teachers? Isn't this a fine, fine school?"

On the weekends—Saturday and Sunday—Tillie climbed her favorite tree,

and she took Beans on walks and threw him sticks,

and she pushed her brother on a swing and tried to teach him how to skip.

But on Mondays and Tuesdays and Wednesdays and Thursdays and Fridays, Tillie went off to school. Beans and her brother did not like to see her go. "Hurry, hurry, hurry home!" her brother called.

One day, Mr. Keene called all the students and teachers together and said, "This is such a fine, fine school! I love this school! Let's have more school! From now on, let's have school on Saturdays, too!"

The teachers and the students did not want to go to school on Saturdays, but no one knew how to tell Mr. Keene that. He was so proud of the children and the teachers, of all the learning they were doing every day.

And so, that Saturday, Tillie set off for school.
"But it's Saturday! What about the swings?"
her brother called.

The following month, Mr. Keene announced, "This is such a fine, fine school! I love this school! Let's have more school! From now on, let's have school on Sundays, too!"

The teachers and the students did not want to go to school on Sundays, but no one knew how to tell Mr. Keene that. He was so proud of the children and the teachers, of all the learning they were doing every day.

And so, that Sunday, Tillie set off for school.

"But it's Sunday! What about the skipping?" her brother called.

The following month, Mr. Keene called everyone together and said, "This is such a fine, fine school! I love this school! Let's have more school! From now on, let's have school on holidays, too—on Easter and Ramadan and Thanksgiving and Christmas and Hanukkah—on all the holidays on every calendar!"

The teachers and the students did not want to go to school on holidays, but no one knew how to tell Mr. Keene that. He was so proud of the children and the teachers, of all the learning they were doing every day.

And so, on Christmas, Tillie set off for school.

"But it's Christmas! What about Christmas?"

her brother called.

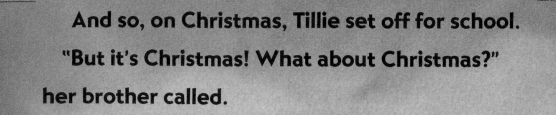

The following month, Mr. Keene called everyone together and said, "This is such a fine, fine school! I love this school! Let's have more school! From now on, let's have school in the summer, too, all summer long, every single day!"

TIME AT HOME (SLEEPING)

...ME IN ...HOOL ...RNING!)

SUMMER SCHEDULE:

JUNE — IS — SCIENCE MONTH!

JULY — IS — BIG WORD ...ONTH!

SUMMER SCHOOL IS COOL

"How much we will learn!" he said. "We can learn everything! We will learn all about numbers and letters, colors and shapes, the Romans and the Egyptians and the Greeks. We will learn about dinosaurs and castles and—and—everything! We will learn *everything*!"

The teachers and the students did not want to go to school on Saturdays and Sundays and holidays and all summer long, every single day. But no one knew how to tell Mr. Keene that. He was so proud of the children and the teachers, of all the learning they were doing every day.

And so, on the first day of summer, Tillie set off for school.
"But it's summer! What about summer?" her brother called.

And that day, Tillie went to see Mr. Keene. She stood in his office, in front of his desk.

"What a fine, fine school this is!" Mr. Keene said. "What amazing things everyone is learning!"

"Yes," Tillie said, "we certainly are learning some amazing things."

"A fine, fine school!" Mr. Keene said.

"But," Tillie said, "not everyone is learning."

"What?" Mr. Keene said. He looked very worried. "Who? Who isn't learning? Tell me, and I will see that they learn!"

"My dog, Beans, hasn't learned how to sit," Tillie said. "And he hasn't learned how to jump over the creek."

"Oh!" Mr. Keene said.

"And my little brother hasn't learned how to swing or skip."

"Oh!" Mr. Keene said.

WRONG WAY, BEANS!

"And I—" she said.

"But you go to school!" Mr. Keene said.

"To our fine, fine school!"

"True," Tillie said. "But I haven't learned how to climb very high in my tree. And I haven't learned how to sit in my tree for a whole hour."

"Oh!" Mr. Keene said.

That day, Mr. Keene walked up and down the halls, looking at the children and the teachers. Up and down he walked. Up and down, up and down.

The next morning, Mr. Keene called everyone together. The children and the teachers were very worried.

Mr. Keene said, "This is a fine, fine school, with fine, fine children and fine, fine teachers. But not everyone is learning."

The children and the teachers were very, very worried.

Mr. Keene said, "There are dogs who need to learn how to sit and how to jump creeks."

What did he mean? Was he going to make their dogs come to school?

"There are little brothers and sisters who need to learn how to swing and how to skip."

What did he mean? Was he going to make their younger brothers and sisters come to school, too?

The children and the teachers were very, very, very worried.

"And you, all of you—children and teachers—you need to learn how to climb a tree and sit in it for an hour!" Mr. Keene said.

The children and the teachers were very worried.

"And so from now on we will . . .

. . . **not** have school on Saturdays or Sundays or holidays or in the summer!"

A huge, enormous, roaring cheer soared up to the ceiling and floated out the windows so that everyone in the town heard the fine, fine children and the fine, fine teachers shout, "Fine! Fine! Fine!"

And the fine, fine children and the fine, fine teachers lifted Mr. Keene up, and they carried him down the hallway and out the doors and through the town, up and down, in and out. And everywhere they went, the people said, "What a fine, fine school with such fine, fine teachers and fine, fine children and a fine, fine principal!"